EUDORA
WELTY

WHY I LIVE AT THE P.O.
AND OTHER STORIES

PENGUIN BOOKS

PENGUIN BOOKS

Published by the Penguin Group. Penguin Books Ltd, 27 Wrights Lane, London W8 5TZ, England. Penguin Books USA Inc., 375 Hudson Street, New York, New York 10014, USA. Penguin Books Australia Ltd, Ringwood, Victoria, Australia. Penguin Books Canada Ltd, 10 Alcorn Avenue, Toronto, Ontario, Canada M4V 3B2. Penguin Books (NZ) Ltd, 182–190 Wairau Road, Auckland 10, New Zealand · Penguin Books Ltd, Registered Offices: Harmondsworth, Middlesex, England · **These stories have been taken from** *The Collected Stories of Eudora Welty*, **first published in Britain by Marion Boyars Publishers in 1981 and published by Penguin Books in 1983.** This edition published 1995 · Copyright 1941, 1949 by Eudora Welty. Copyright in these stories has been renewed. Copyright © Eudora Welty, 1963. All rights reserved · Typeset by Datix International Limited, Bungay, Suffolk. Printed in England by Clays Ltd, St Ives plc · Except in the United States of America, this book is sold subject to the condition that it shall not, by way of trade or otherwise, be lent, re-sold, hired out, or otherwise circulated without the publisher's prior consent in any form of binding or cover other than that in which it is published and without a similar condition including this condition being imposed on the subsequent purchaser ·
10 9 8 7 6 5 4 3 2 1

CONTENTS

Why I Live at the P.O.

I was getting along fine with Mama, Papa-Daddy and Uncle Rondo until my sister Stella-Rondo just separated from her husband and came back home again. Mr Whitaker! Of course I went with Mr Whitaker first, when he first appeared here in China Grove, taking 'Pose Yourself' photos, and Stella-Rondo broke us up. Told him I was one-sided. Bigger on one side than the other, which is a deliberate, calculated falsehood: I'm the same. Stella-Rondo is exactly twelve months to the day younger than I am and for that reason she's spoiled.

She's always had anything in the world she wanted and then she'd throw it away. Papa-Daddy gave her this gorgeous Add-a-Pearl necklace when she was eight years old and she threw it away playing baseball when she was nine, with only two pearls.

So as soon as she got married and moved away from home the first thing she did was separate!

From Mr Whitaker! This photographer with the popeyes she said she trusted. Came home from one of those towns up in Illinois and to our complete surprise brought this child of two.

Mama said she like to made her drop dead for a second. 'Here you had this marvelous blonde child and never so much as wrote your mother a word about it,' says Mama. 'I'm thoroughly ashamed of you.' But of course she wasn't.

Stella-Rondo just calmly takes off this *hat*, I wish you could see it. She says, 'Why, Mama, Shirley-T.'s adopted, I can prove it.'

'How?' says Mama, but all I says was, 'H'm!' There I was over the hot stove, trying to stretch two chickens over five people and a completely unexpected child into the bargain, without one moment's notice.

'What do you mean – "H'm!"?' says Stella-Rondo, and Mama says, 'I heard that, Sister.'

I said that oh, I didn't mean a thing, only that whoever Shirley-T. was, she was the spit-image of Papa-Daddy if he'd cut off his beard, which of course he'd never do in the world. Papa-Daddy's Mama's papa and sulks.

2   Stella-Rondo got furious! She said, 'Sister, I

don't need to tell you you got a lot of nerve and always did have and I'll thank you to make no future reference to my adopted child whatsoever.'

'Very well,' I said. 'Very well, very well. Of course I noticed at once she looks like Mr Whitaker's side too. That frown. She looks like a cross between Mr Whitaker and Papa-Daddy.'

'Well, all I can say is she isn't.'

'She looks exactly like Shirley Temple to me,' says Mama, but Shirley-T. just ran away from her.

So the first thing Stella-Rondo did at the table was turn Papa-Daddy against me.

'Papa-Daddy,' she says. He was trying to cut up his meat. 'Papa-Daddy!' I was taken completely by surprise. Papa-Daddy is about a million years old and's got this long-long beard. 'Papa-Daddy, Sister says she fails to understand why you don't cut off your beard.'

So Papa-Daddy l-a-y-s down his knife and fork! He's real rich. Mama says he is, he says he isn't. So he says, 'Have I heard correctly? You don't understand why I don't cut off my beard?'

'Why,' I says, 'Papa-Daddy, of course I understand, I did not say any such of a thing, the idea!' 3

He says, 'Hussy!'

I says, 'Papa-Daddy, you know I wouldn't any more want you to cut off your beard than the man in the moon. It was the farthest thing from my mind! Stella-Rondo sat there and made that up while she was eating breast of chicken.'

But he says, 'So the postmistress fails to understand why I don't cut off my beard. Which job I got you through my influence with the government. "Bird's nest" – is that what you call it?'

Not that it isn't next to smallest P.O. in the entire state of Mississippi.

I says, 'Oh, Papa-Daddy,' I says, 'I didn't say any such of a thing, I never dreamed it was a bird's nest, I have always been grateful though this is the next to smallest P.O. in the state of Mississippi, and I do not enjoy being referred to as a hussy by my own grandfather.'

But Stella-Rondo says, 'Yes, you did say it too. Anybody in the world could of heard you, that had ears.'

'Stop right there,' says Mama, looking at *me*.

So I pulled my napkin straight back through the napkin ring and left the table.

4   As soon as I was out of the room Mama says,

'Call her back, or she'll starve to death,' but Papa-Daddy says, 'This is the beard I started growing on the Coast when I was fifteen years old.' He would of gone on till nightfall if Shirley-T. hadn't lost the Milky Way she ate in Cairo.

So Papa-Daddy says, 'I am going out and lie in the hammock, and you can all sit here and remember my words: I'll never cut off my beard as long as I live, even one inch, and I don't appreciate it in you at all.' Passed right by me in the hall and went straight out and got in the hammock.

It would be a holiday. It wasn't five minutes before Uncle Rondo suddenly appeared in the hall in one of Stella-Rondo's flesh-colored kimonos, all cut on the bias, like something Mr Whitaker probably thought was gorgeous.

'Uncle Rondo!' I says. 'I didn't know who that was! Where are you going?'

'Sister,' he says, 'get out of my way, I'm poisoned.'

'If you're poisoned stay away from Papa-Daddy,' I says. 'Keep out of the hammock. Papa-Daddy will certainly beat you on the head if you come within forty miles of him. He thinks I deliberately said he ought to cut off his beard 5 after he got me the P.O., and I've told him and told him and told him, and he acts like he just don't hear me. Papa-Daddy must of gone stone deaf.'

'He picked a fine day to do it then,' says Uncle Rondo, and before you could say 'Jack Robinson' flew out in the yard.

What he'd really done, he'd drunk another bottle of that prescription. He does it every single Fourth of July as sure as shooting, and it's horribly expensive. Then he falls over in the hammock and snores. So he insisted on zigzagging right on out to the hammock, looking like a half-wit.

Papa-Daddy woke up with this horrible yell and right there without moving an inch he tried to turn Uncle Rondo against me. I heard every word he said. Oh, he told Uncle Rondo I didn't learn to read till I was eight years old and he didn't see how in the world I ever got the mail put up at the P.O., much less read it all, and he said if Uncle Rondo could only fathom the lengths he had gone to get me that job! And he said on the other hand he thought Stella-Rondo had a brilliant mind and deserved credit for getting out of town. All the time he was just lying there swinging as pretty as you please and looping out his beard, and poor Uncle Rondo was *pleading* with him to slow down the hammock, it was making him as dizzy as a witch to watch it. But that's what Papa-Daddy likes about a hammock. So Uncle Rondo was too dizzy to get turned against me for the time being. He's Mama's only brother and is a good case of a one-track mind. Ask anybody. A certified pharmacist.

Just then I heard Stella-Rondo raising the up-stairs window. While she was married she got this peculiar idea that it's cooler with the windows shut and locked. So she has to raise the window before she can make a soul hear her outdoors.

So she raises a window and says, '*Oh!*' You would have thought she was mortally wounded.

Uncle Rondo and Papa-Daddy didn't even look up, but kept right on with what they were doing. I had to laugh.

I flew up the stairs and threw the door open! I says, 'What in the wide world's the matter, Stella-Rondo? You mortally wounded?'

'No,' she says, 'I am not mortally wounded but I wish you would do me the favor of looking out that window there and telling me what you see.'

So I shade my eyes and look out the window.

'I see the front yard,' I says.

'Don't you see any human beings?' she says.

'I see Uncle Rondo trying to run Papa-Daddy out of the hammock,' I says. 'Nothing more. Naturally, it's so suffocating-hot in the house, with all the windows shut and locked, everybody who cares to stay in their right mind will have to go out and get in the hammock before the Fourth of July is over.'

'Don't you notice anything different about Uncle Rondo?' asks Stella-Rondo.

'Why, no, except he's got on some terrible-looking flesh-colored contraption I wouldn't be found dead in, is all I can see,' I says.

'Never mind, you won't be found dead in it, because it happens to be part of my trousseau, and Mr Whitaker took several dozen photographs of me in it,' says Stella-Rondo. 'What on earth could Uncle Rondo *mean* by wearing part of my trousseau out in the broad open daylight without saying so much as "Kiss my foot," *knowing* I only got home this morning after my separation and hung my negligée up on the bathroom door, just as nervous as I could be?'

'I'm sure I don't know, and what do you expect me to do about it?' I says. 'Jump out the window?'

'No, I expect nothing of the kind. I simply declare that Uncle Rondo looks like a fool in it, that's all,' she says. 'It makes me sick to my stomach.'

'Well, he looks as good as he can,' I says. 'As good as anybody in reason could.' I stood up for Uncle Rondo, please remember. And I said to Stella-Rondo, 'I think I would do well not to criticize so freely if I were you and came home with a two-year-old child I had never said a word about, and no explanation whatever about my separation.'

'I asked you the instant I entered this house not to refer one more time to my adopted child, and you gave me your word of honor you would not,' was all Stella-Rondo would say, and started pulling out every one of her eyebrows with some cheap Kress tweezers.

So I merely slammed the door behind me and went down and made some green-tomato pickle. Somebody had to do it. Of course Mama had turned both the Negroes loose; she always said no 9 earthly power could hold one anyway on the Fourth of July, so she wouldn't even try. It turned out that Jaypan fell in the lake and came within a very narrow limit of drowning.

So Mama trots in. Lifts up the lid and says, 'H'm! Not very good for your Uncle Rondo in his precarious condition, I must say. Oh poor little adopted Shirley-T. Shame on you!'

That made me tired. I says, 'Well, Stella-Rondo had better thank her lucky stars it was her instead of me came trotting in with that very peculiar-looking child. Now if it had been me that trotted in from Illinois and brought a peculiar-looking child of two, I shudder to think of the reception I'd of got, much less controlled the diet of an entire family.'

'But you must remember, Sister, that you were never married to Mr Whitaker in the first place and didn't go up to Illinois to live,' says Mama, shaking a spoon in my face. 'If you had I would of been just as overjoyed to see you and your little adopted girl as I was to see Stella-Rondo, when you wound up with your separation and came on back home.'

'You would not,' I says.

'Don't contradict me, I would,' says Mama.

But I said she couldn't convince me though she talked till she was blue in the face. Then I said, 'Besides, you know as well as I do that that child is not adopted.'

'She most certainly is adopted,' says Mama, stiff as a poker.

I says, 'Why, Mama, Stella-Rondo had her just as sure as anything in this world, and just too stuck up to admit it.'

'Why, Sister,' said Mama. 'Here I thought we were going to have a pleasant Fourth of July, and you start right out not believing a word your own baby sister tells you!'

'Just like Cousin Annie Flo. Went to her grave denying the facts of life,' I remind Mama.

'I told you if you ever mentioned Annie Flo's name I'd slap your face,' says Mama, and slaps my face.

'All right, you wait and see,' I says.

'I,' says Mama, 'I prefer to take my children's word for anything when it's humanly possible.' You ought to see Mama, she weighs two hundred pounds and has real tiny feet.

Just then something perfectly horrible occurred to me.

'Mama,' I says, 'can that child talk?' I simply had to whisper! 'Mama, I wonder if that child can be – you know – in any way? Do you realize,' I says, 'that she hasn't spoken one single, solitary word to a human being up to this minute? This is the way she looks,' I says, and I looked like this.

Well, Mama and I just stood there and stared at each other. It was horrible!

'I remember well that Joe Whitaker frequently drank like a fish,' says Mama. 'I believed to my soul he drank *chemicals*.' And without another word she marches to the foot of the stairs and calls Stella-Rondo.

'Stella-Rondo? O-o-o-o-o! Stella-Rondo!'

'What?' says Stella-Rondo from upstairs. Not even the grace to get up off the bed.

'Can that child of yours talk?' asks Mama.

Stella-Rondo says, 'Can she what?'

'Talk! Talk!' says Mama. 'Burdyburdyburdy-burdy!'

So Stella-Rondo yells back, 'Who says she can't talk?'

'Sister says so,' says Mama.

'You didn't have to tell me, I know whose word

of honor don't mean a thing in this house,' says Stella-Rondo.

And in a minute the loudest Yankee voice I ever heard in my life yells out, 'OE'm Pop-OE the Sailor-r-r-r Ma-a-an!' and then somebody jumps up and down in the upstairs hall. In another second the house would of fallen down.

'Not only talks, she can tap-dance!' calls Stella-Rondo. 'Which is more than some people I won't name can do.'

'Why, the little precious darling thing!' Mama says, so surprised. 'Just as smart as she can be!' Starts talking baby talk right there. Then she turns on me. 'Sister, you ought to be thoroughly ashamed! Run upstairs this instant and apologize to Stella-Rondo and Shirley-T.'

'Apologize for what?' I says. 'I merely wondered if the child was normal, that's all. Now that she's proved she is, why, I have nothing further to say.'

But Mama just turned on her heel and flew out, furious. She ran right upstairs and hugged the baby. She believed it was adopted. Stella-Rondo hadn't done a thing but turn her against me from upstairs while I stood there helpless over the hot 13 stove. So that made Mama, Papa-Daddy and the baby all on Stella-Rondo's side.

Next, Uncle Rondo.

I must say that Uncle Rondo has been marvelous to me at various times in the past and I was completely unprepared to be made to jump out of my skin, the way it turned out. Once Stella-Rondo did something perfectly horrible to him – broke a chain letter from Flanders Field – and he took the radio back he had given her and gave it to me. Stella-Rondo was furious! For six months we all had to call her Stella instead of Stella-Rondo, or she wouldn't answer. I always thought Uncle Rondo had all the brains of the entire family. Another time he sent me to Mammoth Cave, with all expenses paid.

But this would be the day he was drinking that prescription, the Fourth of July.

So at supper Stella-Rondo speaks up and says she thinks Uncle Rondo ought to try to eat a little something. So finally Uncle Rondo said he would try a little cold biscuits and ketchup, but that was all. So *she* brought it to him.

'Do you think it wise to disport with ketchup in Stella-Rondo's flesh-colored kimono?' I says.

Trying to be considerate! If Stella-Rondo couldn't watch out for her trousseau, somebody had to.

'Any objections?' asks Uncle Rondo, just about to pour out all the ketchup.

'Don't mind what she says, Uncle Rondo,' says Stella-Rondo. 'Sister has been devoting this solid afternoon to sneering out my bedroom window at the way you look.'

'What's that?' says Uncle Rondo. Uncle Rondo has got the most terrible temper in the world. Anything is liable to make him tear the house down if it comes at the wrong time.

So Stella-Rondo says, 'Sister says, "Uncle Rondo certainly does look like a fool in that pink kimono!"'

Do you remember who it was really said that?

Uncle Rondo spills out all the ketchup and jumps out of his chair and tears off the kimono and throws it down on the dirty floor and puts his foot on it. It had to be sent all the way to Jackson to the cleaners and re-pleated.

'So that's your opinion of your Uncle Rondo, is it?' he says. 'I look like a fool, do I? Well, that's the last straw. A whole day in this house with nothing to do, and then to hear you come out with a remark like that behind my back!'

'I didn't say any such of a thing, Uncle Rondo,' I says, 'and I'm not saying who did, either. Why, I think you look all right. Just try to take care of yourself and not talk and eat at the same time,' I says. 'I think you better go lie down.'

'Lie down my foot,' says Uncle Rondo. I ought to of known by that he was fixing to do something perfectly horrible.

So he didn't do anything that night in the precarious state he was in – just played Casino with Mama and Stella-Rondo and Shirley-T. and gave Shirley-T. a nickel with a head on both sides. It tickled her nearly to death, and she called him 'Papa'. But at 6.30 a.m. the next morning, he threw a whole five-cent package of some unsold one-inch firecrackers from the store as hard as he could into my bedroom and they every one went off. Not one bad one in the string. Anybody else, there'd be one that wouldn't go off.

Well, I'm just terribly susceptible to noise of any kind, the doctor has always told me I was the most sensitive person he had ever seen in his whole life, and I was simply prostrated. I couldn't eat! People tell me they heard it as far as the cemetery, and old Aunt Jep Patterson, that had been holding her own so good, thought it was Judgment Day and she was going to meet her whole family. It's usually so quiet here.

And I'll tell you it didn't take me any longer than a minute to make up my mind what to do. There I was with the whole entire house on Stella-Rondo's side and turned against me. If I have anything at all I have pride.

So I just decided I'd go straight down to the P.O. There's plenty of room there in the back, I says to myself.

Well! I made no bones about letting the family catch on to what I was up to. I didn't try to conceal it.

The first thing they knew, I marched in where they were all playing Old Maid and pulled the electric oscillating fan out by the plug, and everything got real hot. Next I snatched the pillow I'd done the needle-point on right off the davenport from behind Papa-Daddy. He went 'Ugh!' I beat Stella-Rondo up the stairs and finally found my charm bracelet in her bureau drawer under a picture of Nelson Eddy.

'So that's the way the land lies,' says Uncle Rondo. There he was, piecing on the ham. 'Well,

Sister, I'll be glad to donate my army cot if you got any place to set it up, providing you'll leave right this minute and let me get some peace.' Uncle Rondo was in France.

'Thank you kindly for the cot and "peace" is hardly the word I would select if I had to resort to firecrackers at 6.30 a.m. in a young girl's bed-room,' I says back to him. 'And as to where I intend to go, you seem to forget my position as postmistress of China Grove, Mississippi,' I says. 'I've always got the P.O.'

Well, that made them all sit up and take notice.

I went out front and started digging up some four-o'clocks to plant around the P.O.

'Ah-ah-ah!' says Mama, raising the window. 'Those happen to be my four-o'clocks. Everything planted in that star is mine. I've never known you to make anything grow in your life.'

'Very well,' I says. 'But I take the fern. Even you, Mama, can't stand there and deny that I'm the one watered that fern. And I happen to know where I can send in a box top and get a packet of one thousand mixed seeds, no two the same kind, free.'

18   'Oh, where?' Mama wants to know.

But I says, 'Too late. You 'tend to your house, and I'll 'tend to mine. You hear things like that all the time if you know how to listen to the radio. Perfectly marvelous offers. Get anything you want free.'

So I hope to tell you I marched in and got that radio, and they could of all bit a nail in two, especially Stella-Rondo, that it used to belong to, and she well knew she couldn't get it back, I'd sue for it like a shot. And I very politely took the sewing-machine motor I helped pay the most on to give Mama for Christmas back in 1929, and a good big calendar, with the first-aid remedies on it. The thermometer and the Hawaiian ukulele certainly were rightfully mine, and I stood on the stepladder and got all my watermelon-rind preserves and every fruit and vegetable I'd put up, every jar. Then I began to pull the tacks out of the bluebird wall vases on the archway to the dining room.

'Who told you you could have those, Miss Priss?' says Mama, fanning as hard as she could.

'I bought 'em and I'll keep track of 'em,' I says. 'I'll tack 'em up one on each side the post-office window, and you can see 'em when you come to ask me for your mail, if you're so dead to see 'em.'

'Not I! I'll never darken the door to that post office again if I live to be a hundred,' Mama says. 'Ungrateful child! After all the money we spent on you at the Normal.'

'Me either,' says Stella-Rondo. 'You can just let my mail lie there and *rot*, for all I care. I'll never come and relieve you of a single, solitary piece.'

'I should worry,' I says. 'And who you think's going to sit down and write you those big fat letters and postcards, by the way? Mr Whitaker? Just because he was the only man ever dropped down in China Grove and you got him – unfairly – is he going to sit down and write you a lengthy correspondence after you come home giving no rhyme nor reason whatsoever for your separation and no explanation for the presence of that child? I may not have your brilliant mind, but I fail to see it.'

So Mama says, 'Sister, I've told you a thousand times that Stella-Rondo simply got homesick, and this child is far too big to be hers,' and she says, 'Now, why don't you all just sit down and play Casino?'

Then Shirley-T. sticks out her tongue at me in

this perfectly horrible way. She has no more manners than the man in the moon. I told her she was
going to cross her eyes like that some day and
they'd stick.

'It's too late to stop me now,' I says. 'You
should have tried that yesterday. I'm going to the
P.O. and the only way you can possibly see me is
to visit me there.'

So Papa-Daddy says, 'You'll never catch me
setting foot in that post office, even if I should
take a notion into my head to write a letter some
place.' He says, 'I won't have you reachin' out of
that little old window with a pair of shears and
cuttin' off any beard of mine. I'm too smart for
you!'

'We all are,' says Stella-Rondo.

But I said, 'If you're so smart, where's Mr
Whitaker?'

So then Uncle Rondo says, 'I'll thank you from
now on to stop reading all the orders I get on
postcards and telling everybody in China Grove
what you think is the matter with them,' but I
says, 'I draw my own conclusions and will con-
tinue in the future to draw them.' I says, 'If
people want to write their inmost secrets on penny

postcards, there's nothing in the wide world you can do about it, Uncle Rondo.'

'And if you think we'll ever *write* another post-card you're sadly mistaken,' says Mama.

'Cutting off your nose to spite your face then,' I says. 'But if you're all determined to have no more to do with the U.S. mail, think of this: What will Stella-Rondo do now, if she wants to tell Mr Whitaker to come after her?'

'Wah!' says Stella-Rondo. I knew she'd cry. She had a conniption fit right there in the kitchen.

'It will be interesting to see how long she holds out,' I says. 'And now – I am leaving.'

'Good-bye,' says Uncle Rondo.

'Oh, I declare,' says Mama, 'to think that a family of mine should quarrel on the Fourth of July, or the day after, over Stella-Rondo leaving old Mr Whitaker and having the sweetest little adopted child! It looks like we'd all be glad!'

'Wah!' says Stella-Rondo, and has a fresh con-niption fit.

'*He* left *her* – you mark my words,' I says. 'That's Mr Whitaker. I know Mr Whitaker. After all, I knew him first. I said from the beginning he'd up and leave her. I foretold every single thing that's happened.'

'Where did he go?' asks Mama.

'Probably to the North Pole, if he knows what's good for him,' I says.

But Stella-Rondo just bawled and wouldn't say another word. She flew to her room and slammed the door.

'Now look what you've gone and done, Sister,' says Mama. 'You go apologize.'

'I haven't got time, I'm leaving,' I says.

'Well, what are you waiting around for?' asks Uncle Rondo.

So I just picked up the kitchen clock and marched off, without saying, 'Kiss my foot' or anything, and never did tell Stella-Rondo goodbye.

There was a girl going along on a little wagon right in front.

'Girl,' I says, 'come help me haul these things down the hill, I'm going to live in the post office.'

Took her nine trips in her express wagon. Uncle Rondo came out on the porch and threw her a nickel.

And that's the last I've laid eyes on any of my family or my family laid eyes on me for five solid days and nights. Stella-Rondo may be telling the most horrible tales in the world about Mr Whitaker, but I haven't heard them. As I tell everybody, I draw my own conclusions.

But oh, I like it here. It's ideal, as I've been saying. You see, I've got everything cater-cornered, the way I like it. Hear the radio? All the war news. Radio, sewing machine, book ends, ironing board and that great big piano lamp — peace, that's what I like. Butter-bean vines planted all along the front where the strings are.

Of course, there's not much mail. My family are naturally the main people in China Grove, and if they prefer to vanish from the face of the earth, for all the mail they get or the mail they write, why, I'm not going to open my mouth. Some of the folks here in town are taking up for me and some turned against me. I know which is which. There are always people who will quit buying stamps just to get on the right side of Papa-Daddy.

But here I am, and here I'll stay. I want the world to know I'm happy.

And if Stella-Rondo should come to me this minute, on bended knees, and *attempt* to explain the incidents of her life with Mr Whitaker, I'd simply put my fingers in both my ears and refuse to listen.

R. J. Bowman, who for fourteen years had traveled for a shoe company through Mississippi, drove his Ford along a rutted dirt path. It was a long day! The time did not seem to clear the noon hurdle and settle into soft afternoon. The sun, keeping its strength here even in winter, stayed at the top of the sky, and every time Bowman stuck his head out of the dusty car to stare up the road, it seemed to reach a long arm down and push against the top of his head, right through his hat – like the practical joke of an old drummer, long on the road. It made him feel all the more angry and helpless. He was feverish, and he was not quite sure of the way.

This was his first day back on the road after a long siege of influenza. He had had very high fever, and dreams, and had become weakened and pale, enough to tell the difference in the mirror, and he could not think clearly . . . All afternoon, in the midst of his anger, and for no reason, he had thought of his dead grandmother. She had been a comfortable soul. Once more Bowman wished he could fall into the big feather bed that had been in her room ... Then he forgot her again.

This desolate hill country! And he seemed to be going the wrong way – it was as if he were going back, far back. There was not a house in sight ... There was no use wishing he were back in bed, though. By paying the hotel doctor his bill he had proved his recovery. He had not even been sorry when the pretty trained nurse said good-bye. He did not like illness, he distrusted it, as he distrusted the road without signposts. It angered him. He had given the nurse a really expensive bracelet, just because she was packing up her bag and leaving.

But now – what if in fourteen years on the road he had never been ill before and never had an accident? His record was broken, and he had even begun almost to question it ... He had gradually put up at better hotels, in the bigger towns, but weren't they all, eternally, stuffy in summer and drafty in winter? Women? He could only remember little rooms within little rooms, like a nest of 27

Chinese paper boxes, and if he thought of one woman he saw the worn loneliness that the furniture of that room seemed built of. And he himself – he was a man who always wore rather wide-brimmed black hats, and in the wavy hotel mirrors had looked something like a bullfighter, as he paused for that inevitable instant on the landing, walking downstairs to supper . . . He leaned out of the car again, and once more the sun pushed at his head.

Bowman had wanted to reach Beulah by dark, to go to bed and sleep off his fatigue. As he remembered, Beulah was fifty miles away from the last town, on a graveled road. This was only a cow trail. How had he ever come to such a place? One hand wiped the sweat from his face, and he drove on.

He had made the Beulah trip before. But he had never seen this hill or this petering-out path before – or that cloud, he thought shyly, looking up and then down quickly – any more than he had seen this day before. Why did he not admit he was simply lost and had been for miles? . . . He was not in the habit of asking the way of strangers, and these people never knew where the very roads they lived on went to; but then he had not even been close enough to anyone to call out. People standing in the fields now and then, or on top of the haystacks, had been too far away, looking like leaning sticks or weeds, turning a little at the solitary rattle of his car across their countryside, watching the pale sobered winter dust where it chunked out behind like big squashes down the road. The stares of these distant people had followed him solidly like a wall, impenetrable, behind which they turned back after he had passed.

The cloud floated there to one side like the bolster on his grandmother's bed. It went over a cabin on the edge of a hill, where two bare chinaberry trees clutched at the sky. He drove through a heap of dead oak leaves, his wheels stirring their weightless sides to make a silvery melancholy whistle as the car passed through their bed. No car had been along this way ahead of him. Then he saw that he was on the edge of a ravine that fell away, a red erosion, and that this was indeed the road's end.

He pulled the brake. But it did not hold, though he put all his strength into it. The car, tipped toward the edge, rolled a little. Without a doubt, it was going over the bank.

He got out quietly, as though some mischief had been done him and he had his dignity to remember. He lifted his bag and sample case out, set them down, and stood back and watched the car roll over the edge. He heard something – not the crash he was listening for, but a slow, un-uproarious crackle. Rather distastefully he went to look over, and he saw that his car had fallen into a tangle of immense grapevines as thick as his arm, which caught it and held it, rocked it like a grotesque child in a dark cradle, and then, as he watched, concerned somehow that he was not still inside it, released it gently to the ground.

He sighed.

Where am I? he wondered with a shock. Why didn't I do something? All his anger seemed to have drifted away from him. There was the house, back on the hill. He took a bag in each hand and with almost childlike willingness went toward it. But his breathing came with difficulty, and he had to stop to rest.

It was a shotgun house, two rooms and an open passage between, perched on the hill. The whole cabin slanted a little under the heavy heaped-up vine that covered the roof, light and green, as though forgotten from summer. A woman stood in the passage.

He stopped still. Then all of a sudden his heart began to behave strangely. Like a rocket set off, it began to leap and expand into uneven patterns of beats which showered into his brain, and he could not think. But in scattering and falling it made no noise. It shot up with great power, almost elation, and fell gently, like acrobats into nets. It began to pound profoundly, then waited irresponsibly, hitting in some sort of inward mockery first at his ribs, then against his eyes, then under his shoulder blades, and against the roof of his mouth when he tried to say, 'Good afternoon, madam.' But he could not hear his heart – it was as quiet as ashes falling. This was rather comforting; still, it was shocking to Bowman to feel his heart beating at all.

Stock-still in his confusion, he dropped his bags, which seemed to drift in slow bulks gracefully through the air and to cushion themselves on the gray prostrate grass near the doorstep.

As for the woman standing there, he saw at once that she was old. Since she could not possibly hear his heart, he ignored the pounding and now looked at her carefully, and yet in his distraction dreamily, with his mouth open.

She had been cleaning the lamp, and held it, half blackened, half clear, in front of her. He saw her with the dark passage behind her. She was a big woman with a weather-beaten but unwrinkled face; her lips were held tightly together, and her eyes looked with a curious dulled brightness into his. He looked at her shoes, which were like bundles. If it were summer she would be barefoot . . . Bowman, who automatically judged a woman's age on sight, set her at fifty. She wore a formless garment of some gray coarse material, rough-dried from a washing, from which her arms appeared pink and unexpectedly round. When she never said a word, and sustained her quiet pose of holding the lamp, he was convinced of the strength in her body.

'Good afternoon, madam,' he said.

She stared on, whether at him or at the air around him he could not tell, but after a moment she lowered her eyes to show that she would listen to whatever he had to say.

'I wonder if you would be interested –' He tried once more. 'An accident – my car . . .'

Her voice emerged low and remote, like a sound across a lake. 'Sonny he ain't here.'

'Sonny?'

'Sonny ain't here now.'

Her son – a fellow able to bring my car up, he decided in blurred relief. He pointed down the hill. 'My car's in the bottom of the ditch. I'll need help.'

'Sonny ain't here, but he'll be here.'

She was becoming clearer to him and her voice stronger, and Bowman saw that she was stupid.

He was hardly surprised at the deepening postponement and tedium of his journey. He took a breath, and heard his voice speaking over the silent blows of his heart. 'I was sick. I am not strong yet . . . May I come in?'

He stooped and laid his big black hat over the handle on his bag. It was a humble motion, almost a bow, that instantly struck him as absurd and betraying of all his weakness. He looked up at the woman, the wind blowing his hair. He might have continued for a long time in this unfamiliar attitude; he had never been a patient man, but when he was sick he had learned to sink submissively into the pillows, to wait for his medicine. He waited on the woman.

Then she, looking at him with blue eyes, turned and held open the door, and after a moment Bowman, as if convinced in his action, stood erect and followed her in.

Inside, the darkness of the house touched him like a professional hand, the doctor's. The woman set the half-cleaned lamp on a table in the center of the room and pointed, also like a professional person, a guide, to a chair with a yellow cowhide seat. She herself crouched on the hearth, drawing her knees up under the shapeless dress.

At first he felt hopefully secure. His heart was quieter. The room was enclosed in the gloom of yellow pine boards. He could see the other room, with the foot of an iron bed showing, across the passage. The bed had been made up with a red-and-yellow pieced quilt that looked like a map or a picture, a little like his grandmother's girlhood painting of Rome burning.

He had ached for coolness, but in this room it was cold. He stared at the hearth with dead coals lying on it and iron pots in the corners. The hearth and smoked chimney were of the stone he had seen ribbing the hills, mostly slate. Why is there no fire? he wondered.

And it was so still. The silence of the fields seemed to enter and move familiarly through the house. The wind used the open hall. He felt that he was in a mysterious, quiet, cool danger. It was necessary to do what? . . . To talk.

'I have a nice line of women's low-priced shoes . . .' he said.

But the woman answered, 'Sonny'll be here. He's strong. Sonny'll move your car.'

'Where is he now?'

'Farms for Mr Redmond.'

Mr Redmond. Mr Redmond. That was someone he would never have to encounter, and he was glad. Somehow the name did not appeal to him . . . In a flare of touchiness and anxiety, Bowman wished to avoid even mention of unknown men and their unknown farms.

'Do you two live here alone?' He was surprised to hear his old voice, chatty, confidential, inflected for selling shoes, asking a question like that – a thing he did not even want to know.

'Yes. We are alone.'

He was surprised at the way she answered. She

had taken a long time to say that. She had nodded her head in a deep way too. Had she wished to affect him with some sort of premonition? he wondered unhappily. Or was it only that she would not help him, after all, by talking with him? For he was not strong enough to receive the impact of unfamiliar things without a little talk to break their fall. He had lived a month in which nothing had happened except in his head and his body – an almost inaudible life of heartbeats and dreams that came back, a life of fever and privacy, a delicate life which had left him weak to the point of – what? Of begging. The pulse in his palm leapt like a trout in a brook.

He wondered over and over why the woman did not go ahead with cleaning the lamp. What prompted her to stay there across the room, silently bestowing her presence upon him? He saw that with her it was not a time for doing little tasks. Her face was grave; she was feeling how right she was. Perhaps it was only politeness. In docility he held his eyes stiffly wide; they fixed themselves on the woman's clasped hands as though she held the cord they were strung on.

36   Then, 'Sonny's coming,' she said.

He himself had not heard anything, but there came a man passing the window and then plunging in at the door, with two hounds beside him. Sonny was a big enough man, with his belt slung low about his hips. He looked at least thirty. He had a hot, red face that was yet full of silence. He wore muddy blue pants and an old military coat stained and patched. World War? Bowman wondered. Great God, it was a Confederate coat. On the back of his light hair he had a wide filthy black hat which seemed to insult Bowman's own. He pushed down the dogs from his chest. He was strong, with dignity and heaviness in his way of moving . . . There was the resemblance to his mother.

They stood side by side . . . He must account again for his presence here.

'Sonny, this man, he had his car to run off over the prec'pice an' wants to know if you will git it out for him,' the woman said after a few minutes.

Bowman could not even state his case.

Sonny's eyes lay upon him.

He knew he should offer explanations and show money – at least appear either penitent or authoritative. But all he could do was to shrug slightly.

Sonny brushed by him going to the window,

followed by the eager dogs, and looked out. There was effort even in the way he was looking, as if he could throw his sight out like a rope. Without turning Bowman felt that his own eyes could have seen nothing: it was too far.

'Got me a mule out there an' got me a block an' tackle,' said Sonny meaningfully. 'I *could* catch me my mule an' git me my ropes, an' before long I'd git your car out the ravine.'

He looked completely around the room, as if in meditation, his eyes roving in their own distance. Then he pressed his lips firmly and yet shyly together, and with the dogs ahead of him this time, he lowered his head and strode out. The hard earth sounded, cupping to his powerful way of walking – almost a stagger.

Mischievously, at the suggestion of those sounds, Bowman's heart leapt again. It seemed to walk about inside him.

'Sonny's goin' to do it,' the woman said. She said it again, singing it almost, like a song. She was sitting in her place by the hearth.

Without looking out, he heard some shouts and the dogs barking and the pounding of hoofs in short runs on the hill. In a few minutes Sonny passed under the window with a rope, and there was a brown mule with quivering, shining, purple-looking ears. The mule actually looked in the window. Under its eyelashes it turned target-like eyes into his. Bowman averted his head and saw the woman looking serenely back at the mule, with only satisfaction in her face.

She sang a little more, under her breath. It occurred to him, and it seemed quite marvelous, that she was not really talking to him, but rather following the thing that came about with words that were unconscious and part of her looking.

So he said nothing, and this time when he did not reply he felt a curious and strong emotion, not fear, rise up in him.

This time, when his heart leapt, something – his soul – seemed to leap too, like a little colt invited out of a pen. He stared at the woman while the frantic nimbleness of his feeling made his head sway. He could not move; there was nothing he could do, unless perhaps he might embrace this woman who sat there growing old and shapeless before him.

But he wanted to leap up, to say to her, I have been sick and I found out then, only then, how 39 lonely I am. Is it too late? My heart puts up a struggle inside me, and you may have heard it, protesting against emptiness . . . It should be full, he would rush on to tell her, thinking of his heart now as a deep lake, it should be holding love like other hearts. It should be flooded with love. There would be a warm spring day . . . Come and stand in my heart, whoever you are, and a whole river would cover your feet and rise higher and take your knees in whirlpools, and draw you down to itself, your whole body, your heart too.

But he moved a trembling hand across his eyes, and looked at the placid crouching woman across the room. She was still as a statue. He felt ashamed and exhausted by the thought that he might, in one more moment, have tried by simple words and embraces to communicate some strange thing – something which seemed always to have just escaped him . . .

Sunlight touched the furthest pot on the hearth. It was late afternoon. This time tomorrow he would be somewhere on a good graveled road, driving his car past things that happened to people, quicker than their happening. Seeing ahead to the next day, he was glad, and knew that this was no time to embrace an old woman. He could feel in his pounding temples the readying of his blood for motion and for hurrying away.

'Sonny's hitched up your car by now,' said the woman. 'He'll git it out the ravine right shortly.'

'Fine!' he cried with his customary enthusiasm.

Yet it seemed a long time that they waited. It began to get dark. Bowman was cramped in his chair. Any man should know enough to get up and walk around while he waited. There was something like guilt in such stillness and silence.

But instead of getting up, he listened ... His breathing restrained, his eyes powerless in the growing dark, he listened uneasily for a warning sound, forgetting in wariness what it would be. Before long he heard something – soft, continuous, insinuating.

'What's that noise?' he asked, his voice jumping into the dark. Then wildly he was afraid it would be his heart beating so plainly in the quiet room, and she would tell him so.

'You might hear the stream,' she said grudgingly.

Her voice was closer. She was standing by the 41

table. He wondered why she did not light the lamp. She stood there in the dark and did not light it.

Bowman would never speak to her now, for the time was past. I'll sleep in the dark, he thought, in his bewilderment pitying himself.

Heavily she moved on to the window. Her arm, vaguely white, rose straight from her full side and she pointed out into the darkness.

'That white speck's Sonny,' she said, talking to herself.

He turned unwillingly and peered over her shoulder; he hesitated to rise and stand beside her. His eyes searched the dusky air. The white speck floated smoothly toward her finger, like a leaf on a river, growing whiter in the dark. It was as if she had shown him something secret, part of her life, but had offered no explanation. He looked away. He was moved almost to tears, feeling for no reason that she had made a silent declaration equivalent to his own. His hand waited upon his chest.

Then a step shook the house, and Sonny was in the room. Bowman felt how the woman left him there and went to the other man's side.

'I done got your car out, mister,' said Sonny's voice in the dark. 'She's settin' a-waitin' in the road, turned to go back where she come from.'

'Fine!' said Bowman, projecting his own voice to loudness. 'I'm surely much obliged – I could never have done it myself – I was sick . . .'

'I could do it easy,' said Sonny.

Bowman could feel them both waiting in the dark, and he could hear the dogs panting out in the yard, waiting to bark when he should go. He felt strangely helpless and resentful. Now that he could go, he longed to stay. Of what was he being deprived? His chest was rudely shaken by the violence of his heart. These people cherished something here that he could not see, they withheld some ancient promise of food and warmth and light. Between them they had a conspiracy. He thought of the way she had moved away from him and gone to Sonny, she had flowed toward him. He was shaking with cold, he was tired, and it was not fair. Humbly and yet angrily he stuck his hand into his pocket.

'Of course I'm going to pay you for everything –'

'We don't take money for such,' said Sonny's voice belligerently.

'I want to pay. But do something more . . . Let

me stay – tonight . . .' He took another step toward them. If only they could see him, they would know his sincerity, his real need! His voice went on, 'I'm not very strong yet, I'm not able to walk far, even back to my car, maybe, I don't know – I don't know exactly where I am –'

He stopped. He felt as if he might burst into tears. What would they think of him!

Sonny came over and put his hands on him. Bowman felt them pass (they were professional too) across his chest, over his hips. He could feel Sonny's eyes upon him in the dark.

'You ain't no revenuer come sneakin' here, mister, ain't got no gun?'

To this end of nowhere! And yet *he* had come. He made a grave answer. 'No.'

'You can stay.'

'Sonny,' said the woman, 'you'll have to borry some fire.'

'I'll go git it from Redmond's,' said Sonny.

'What?' Bowman strained to hear their words to each other.

'Our fire, it's out, and Sonny's got to borry some, because it's dark an' cold,' she said.

'But matches – I have matches –'

'We don't have no need for 'em,' she said proudly. 'Sonny's goin' after his own fire.'

'I'm goin' to Redmond's,' said Sonny with an air of importance, and he went out.

After they had waited a while, Bowman looked out the window and saw a light moving over the hill. It spread itself out like a little fan. It zigzagged along the field, darting and swift, not like Sonny at all . . . Soon enough, Sonny staggered in, holding a burning stick behind him in tongs, fire flowing in his wake, blazing light into the corners of the room.

'We'll make a fire now,' the woman said, taking the brand.

When that was done she lit the lamp. It showed its dark and light. The whole room turned golden-yellow like some sort of flower, and the walls smelled of it and seemed to tremble with the quiet rushing of the fire and the waving of the burning lampwick in its funnel of light.

The woman moved among the iron pots. With the tongs she dropped hot coals on top of the iron lids. They made a set of soft vibrations, like the sound of a bell far away.

She looked up and over at Bowman, but he could not answer. He was trembling . . .

'Have a drink, mister?' Sonny asked. He had brought in a chair from the other room and sat astride it with his folded arms across the back. Now we are all visible to one another, Bowman thought, and cried, 'Yes sir, you bet, thanks!'

'Come after me and do just what I do,' said Sonny.

It was another excursion into the dark. They went through the hall, out to the back of the house, past a shed and a hooded well. They came to a wilderness of thicket.

'Down on your knees,' said Sonny.

'What?' Sweat broke out on his forehead.

He understood when Sonny began to crawl through a sort of tunnel that the bushes made over the ground. He followed, startled in spite of himself when a twig or a thorn touched him gently without making a sound, clinging to him and finally letting him go.

Sonny stopped crawling and, crouched on his knees, began to dig with both his hands into the dirt. Bowman shyly struck matches and made a light. In a few minutes Sonny pulled up a jug. He poured out some of the whisky into a bottle from his coat pocket, and buried the jug again. 'You never know who's liable to knock at your door,' he said, and laughed. 'Start back,' he said, almost formally. 'Ain't no need for us to drink outdoors, like hogs.'

At the table by the fire, sitting opposite each other in their chairs, Sonny and Bowman took drinks out of the bottle, passing it across. The dogs slept; one of them was having a dream.

'This is good,' said Bowman. 'This is what I needed.' It was just as though he were drinking the fire off the hearth.

'He makes it,' said the woman with quiet pride.

She was pushing the coals off the pots, and the smells of corn bread and coffee circled the room. She set everything on the table before the men, with a bone-handled knife stuck into one of the potatoes, splitting out its golden fiber. Then she stood for a minute looking at them, tall and full above them where they sat. She leaned a little toward them.

'You all can eat now,' she said, and suddenly smiled.

Bowman had just happened to be looking at her. He set his cup back on the table in unbelieving protest. A pain pressed at his eyes. He saw that she was not an old woman. She was young, still young. He could think of no number of years for her. She was the same age as Sonny, and she belonged to him. She stood with the deep dark corner of the room behind her, the shifting yellow light scattering over her head and her gray formless dress, trembling over her tall body when it bent over them in its sudden communication. She was young. Her teeth were shining and her eyes glowed. She turned and walked slowly and heavily out of the room, and he heard her sit down on the cot and then lie down. The pattern on the quilt moved.

'She's goin' to have a baby,' said Sonny, popping a bite into his mouth.

Bowman could not speak. He was shocked with knowing what was really in this house. A marriage, a fruitful marriage. That simple thing. Anyone could have had that.

Somehow he felt unable to be indignant or protest, although some sort of joke had certainly been played upon him. There was nothing remote or mysterious here – only something private. The only secret was the ancient communication between two people. But the memory of the woman's waiting silently by the cold hearth, of the man's stubborn journey a mile away to get fire, and how they finally brought out their food and drink and filled the room proudly with all they had to show, was suddenly too clear and too enormous within him for response . . .

'You ain't as hungry as you look,' said Sonny.

The woman came out of the bedroom as soon as the men had finished, and ate her supper while her husband stared peacefully into the fire.

Then they put the dogs out, with the food that was left.

'I think I'd better sleep here by the fire, on the floor,' said Bowman.

He felt that he had been cheated, and that he could afford now to be generous. Ill though he was, he was not going to ask them for their bed. He was through with asking favors in this house, now that he understood what was there.

'Sure, mister.'

But he had not known yet how slowly he understood. They had not meant to give him their bed.

After a little interval they both rose and looking at him gravely went into the other room.

He lay stretched by the fire until it grew low and dying. He watched every tongue of blaze lick out and vanish. 'There will be special reduced prices on all footwear during the month of January,' he found himself repeating quietly, and then he lay with his lips tight shut.

How many noises the night had! He heard the stream running, the fire dying, and he was sure now that he heard his heart beating, too, the sound it made under his ribs. He heard breathing, round and deep, of the man and his wife in the room across the passage. And that was all. But emotion swelled patiently within him, and he wished that the child were his.

He must get back to where he had been before. He stood weakly before the red coals and put on his overcoat. It felt too heavy on his shoulders. As he started out he looked and saw that the woman had never got through with cleaning the lamp. On some impulse he put all the money from his billfold under its fluted glass base, almost ostentatiously.

Ashamed, shrugging a little, and then shivering,

he took his bags and went out. The cold of the air seemed to lift him bodily. The moon was in the sky.

On the slope he began to run, he could not help it. Just as he reached the road, where his car seemed to sit in the moonlight like a boat, his heart began to give off tremendous explosions like a rifle, bang bang bang.

He sank in fright on to the road, his bags falling about him. He felt as if all this had happened before. He covered his heart with both hands to keep anyone from hearing the noise it made.

But nobody heard it.

That was Miss Snowdie MacLain.

She comes after her butter, won't let me run over with it from just across the road. Her husband walked out of the house one day and left his hat on the banks of the Big Black River. – That could have started something, too.

We might have had a little run on doing that in Morgana, if it had been so willed. What King did, the copy-cats always might do. Well King MacLain left a new straw hat on the banks of the Big Black and there are people that consider he headed West.

Snowdie grieved for him, but the decent way you'd grieve for the dead, more like, and nobody wanted to think, around her, that he treated her that way. But how long can you humor the humored? Well, always. But I could almost bring myself to talk about it – to a passer-by, that will never see her again, or me either. Sure I can churn and talk. My name's Mrs Rainey.

You seen she wasn't ugly – and the little blinky lines to her eyelids comes from trying to see. She's an albino but nobody would ever try to call her ugly around here – with that tender, tender skin like a baby. Some said King figured out that if the babies started coming, he had a chance for a nestful of little albinos, and that swayed him. No, I don't say it. I say he was just willful. *He* wouldn't think ahead.

Willful and outrageous, to some several. Well: he married Snowdie.

Lots of worse men wouldn't have: no better sense. Them Hudsons had more than MacLains, but none of 'em had enough to count or worry over. Not by then. Hudson money built that house, and built it for *Snowdie* ... they prayed over that. But take King: marrying must have been some of his showing off – like man never married at all till *he* flung in, then had to show the others how he could go right on acting. And like, 'Look, everybody, this is what I think of Morgana and MacLain Courthouse and all the way between' – further, for all I know – 'marrying a girl with pink eyes'. 'I swan!' we all say. Just like he wants us to, scoundrel. And Snowdie as sweet and gentle as you find them. Of course, gentle people aren't the ones you lead best, he had that to find out, so know-all. No, sir, she'll beat him yet, balking. In the meantime children of his growing up in the County Orphans', so say several, and children known and unknown, scattered-like. When he does come, he's just as nice as he can be to Snowdie. Just as courteous. Was from the start.

Haven't you noticed it prevail, in the world in general? Beware of a man with manners. He never raised his voice to her, but then one day he walked out of the house. Oh, I don't mean once!

He went away for a good spell before he come back that time. She had a little story about him needing the waters. Next time it was more than a year, it was two – oh, it was three. I had two children myself, enduring his being gone, and one to die. Yes, and that time he sent her word ahead: 'Meet me in the woods.' No, he more invited her than told her to come – 'Suppose you meet me in the woods.' And it was nighttime he supposed to her. And Snowdie met him without asking 'What for?' which I would want to know of Fate Rainey. After all, they were married — they had a right to

54 sit inside and talk in the light and comfort, or lie

down easy on a good goosefeather bed, either. I would even consider he might not be there when I came. Well, if Snowdie went without question, then I can tell it without a question as long as I love Snowdie. Her version is that in the woods they met and both decided on what would be best.

Best for him, of course. We could see the writing on the wall.

'The woods' was Morgan's Woods. We would any of us know the place he meant, without trying – I could have streaked like an arrow to the very oak tree, one there to itself and all spready: a real shady place by *day*, is all I know. Can't you just see King MacLain leaning his length against that tree by the light of the moon as you come walking through Morgan's Woods and you hadn't seen him in three years? 'Suppose you meet me in the woods.' My foot. Oh, I don't know how poor Snowdie stood it, crossing the distance.

Then, twins.

That was where I come in, I could help when things got to there. I took her a little churning of butter with her milk and we took up. I hadn't been married long myself, and Mr Rainey's health was already a little delicate so he'd thought best to quit heavy work. We was both hard workers fairly early.

I always thought twins might be nice. And might have been for them, by just the sound of it. The MacLains first come to Morgana bride and groom from MacLain and went into that new house. He was educated off, to practice law – well needed here. Snowdie was Miss Lollie Hudson's daughter, well known. Her father was Mr Eugene Hudson, a storekeeper down at Crossroads past the Courthouse, but he was a lovely man. Snowdie was their only daughter, and they give her a nice education. And I guess people more or less expected her to teach school: not marry. She couldn't see all that well, was the only thing in the way, but Mr Comus Stark here and the supervisors overlooked that, knowing the family and Snowdie's real good way with Sunday School children. Then before the school year even got a good start, she got took up by King MacLain all of a sudden. I think it was when jack-o'-lanterns was pasted on her window I used to see his buggy roll up right to the school-house steps and wait on her. He courted her in Morgana and MacLain too, both ends, didn't skip a day.

It was no different – no quicker and no slower – than the like happens every whipstitch, so I don't need to tell you they got married in the MacLain Presbyterian Church before you could shake a stick at it, no matter how surprised people were going to be. And once they dressed Snowdie all in white, you know she was whiter than your dreams.

So – he'd been educated in the law and he traveled for somebody, that was the first thing he did – I'll tell you in a minute what he sold, and she stayed home and cooked and kept house. I forget if she had a Negro, she didn't know how to tell one what to do if she had. And she put her eyes straight out, almost, going to work and making curtains for every room and all like that. So busy. At first it didn't look like they would have any children.

So it went the way I told you, slipped into it real easy, people took it for granted mighty early – him leaving and him being welcomed home, him leaving and him sending word, 'Meet me in the woods', and him gone again, at last leaving the hat. I told my husband I was going to quit keeping count of King's comings and goings, and 57 it wasn't long after that he did leave the hat. I don't know yet whether he meant it kind or cruel. Kind, I incline to believe. Or maybe she was winning. Why do I try to figure? Maybe because Fate Rainey ain't got a surprise in him, and proud of it. So Fate said, 'Well now, let's have the women to settle down and pay attention to home-folks a while.' That was all he could say about it.

So, you wouldn't have had to wait long. Here comes Snowdie across the road to bring the news. I seen her coming across my pasture in a different walk, it was the way somebody comes down an aisle. Her sun-bonnet ribbons was jumping around her: springtime. Did you notice her little dainty waist she has still? I declare it's a mystery to think about her having the strength once. Look at me.

I was in the barn milking, and she come and took a stand there at the head of the little Jersey, Lady May. She had a quiet, picked-out way to tell news. She said, 'I'm going to have a baby too, Miss Katie. Congratulate me.'

Me and Lady May both had to just stop and look at her. She looked like more than only the news had come over her. It was like a shower of something had struck her, like she'd been caught out in something bright. It was more than the day. There with her eyes all crinkled up with always fighting the light, yet she was looking out bold as a lion that day under her brim, and gazing into my bucket and into my stall like a visiting somebody. Poor Snowdie. I remember it was Easter time and how the pasture was all spotty there behind her little blue skirt, in sweet clover. He sold tea and spices, that's what it was.

It was sure enough nine months to the day the twins come after he went sallying out through those woods and fields and laid his hat down on the bank of the river with 'King MacLain' on it.

I wish I'd seen him! I don't guess I'd have stopped him. I can't tell you why, but I wish I'd seen him! But nobody did.

For Snowdie's sake – here they come bringing the hat, and a hullaballoo raised – they drug the Big Black for nine miles down, or was it only eight, and sent word to Bovina and on, clear to Vicksburg, to watch out for anything to wash up or to catch in the trees in the river. Sure, there never was anything – just the hat. They found everybody else that ever honestly drowned along the Big Black in this neighborhood. Mr Sissum at the store, he drowned later on and they found him. I think with the hat he ought to have laid his watch down, if he wanted to give it a better look.

Snowdie kept just as bright and brave, she didn't seem to give in. She must have had her thoughts and they must have been one of two things. One that he was dead – then why did her face have the glow? It had a glow – and the other that he left her and meant it. And like people said, if she smiled *then*, she was clear out of reach. I didn't know if I liked the glow. Why didn't she rage and storm a little – to me, anyway, just Mrs Rainey? The Hudsons all hold themselves in. But it didn't seem to me, running in and out the way I was, that Snowdie had ever got a real good look at life, maybe. Maybe from the beginning. Maybe she just doesn't know the *extent*. Not the kind of look I got, and away back when I was twelve year old or so. Like something was put to my eye.

She just went on keeping house, and getting fairly big with what I told you already was twins, and she seemed to settle into her content. Like a little white kitty in a basket, making you wonder if she just mightn't put up her paw and scratch, if anything was, after all, to come near. At her house it was like Sunday even in the mornings, every day, in that cleaned-up way. She was taking a joy in her fresh untracked rooms and that dark, quiet, real quiet hall that runs through her house. And I love Snowdie. I love her.

Except none of us felt very *close* to her all the while. I'll tell you what it was, what made her different. It was the not waiting any more, except where the babies waited, and that's not but one story. We were mad at her and protecting her all at once, when we couldn't be close to her.

And she come out in her pretty clean shirtwaists to water the ferns, and she had remarkable flowers – she had her mother's way with flowers, of course. And give just as many away, except it wasn't like I or you give. She was by her own self. Oh, her mother was dead by then, and Mr Hudson fourteen miles down the road away, crippled up, running his store in a cane chair. We was every bit she had. Everybody tried to stay with her as much as they could spare, not let a day go by without one of us to run in and speak to her and say a word about an ordinary thing. Miss Lizzie Stark let her be in charge of raising money for the poor country people at Christmas that year, and 61 like that. Of course we made all her little things for her, stitches like that was way beyond her. It was a good thing she got such a big stack.

The twins come the first day of January. Miss Lizzie Stark – she hates all men, and is real important: across yonder's her chimney – made Mr Comus Stark, her husband, hitch up and drive to Vicksburg to bring back a Vicksburg doctor in her own buggy the night before, instead of using Dr Loomis here, and stuck him in a cold room to sleep at her house; she said trust any doctor's buggy to break down on those bridges. Mrs Stark stayed right by Snowdie, and of course several, and I, stayed too, but Mrs Stark was not budging and took charge when pains commenced. Snowdie had the two little boys and neither one albino. They were both King all over again, if you want to know it. Mrs Stark had so hoped for a girl, or two *girls*. Snowdie clapped the names on them of Lucius Randall and Eugene Hudson, after her own father and her mother's father.

It was the only sign she ever give Morgana that maybe she didn't think the name King MacLain had stayed beautiful. But not much of a sign; some women don't name after their husbands, until they get down to nothing else left. I don't think with Snowdie even *two* other names meant she had changed yet, not towards King, that scoundrel.

Time goes like a dream no matter how hard you run, and all the time we heard things from out in the world that we listened to but that still didn't mean we believed them. You know the kind of things. Somebody's cousin saw King MacLain. Mr Comus Stark, the one the cotton and timber belongs to, he goes a little, and he claimed three or four times he saw his back, and once saw him getting a haircut in Texas. Those things you will hear forever when people go off, to keep up a few shots in the woods. They might mean something – might not.

Till the most outrageous was the time my husband went up to Jackson. He saw a man that was the spit-image of King in the parade, my husband told me in his good time, the inauguration of Governor Vardaman. He was right up with the big ones and astride a fine animal. Several from here went but as Mrs Spight said, why wouldn't they be looking at the Governor? Or the New Capitol? But King MacLain could steal anyone's glory, so he thought. 63

When I asked the way he looked, I couldn't get a thing out of my husband, except he lifted his feet across the kitchen floor like a horse and man in one, and I went after him with my broom. I knew, though. If it was King, he looked like, 'Hasn't everybody been wondering, though, been out of their minds to know, where I've been keeping myself!' I told my husband it reasoned to me like it was up to Governor Vardaman to get hold of King and bring something out of him, but my husband said why pick on one man, and besides a parade was going on and what all. Men! I said if I'd been Governor Vardaman and spied King MacLain from Morgana marching in my parade as big as I was and no call for it, I'd have had the whole thing brought to a halt and called him to accounts. 'Well, what good would it have done you?' my husband said. 'A plenty,' I said. I was excited at the time it happened. 'That was just as good a spot as any to show him forth, right in front of the New Capitol in Jackson with the band going, and just as good a man to do it.'

Well, sure, men like that need to be shown up before the world, I guess – not that any of us would be surprised. 'Did you go and find him

after the Governor got inaugurated to suit you then?'
I asked my husband. But he said no, and reminded
me. He went for me a new bucket; and brought me
the wrong size. Just like the ones at Holifield's. But
he said he saw King or his twin. What twin!

Well, through the years, we'd hear of him here
or there – maybe two places at once, New Orleans
and Mobile. That's people's careless way of using
their eyes.

I believe he's been to California. Don't ask me
why. But I picture him there. I see King in the
West, out where it's gold and all that. Everybody
to their own visioning.

II

Well, what happened turned out to happen on
Hallowe'en. Only last week – and seems already
like something that couldn't happen at all.

My baby girl, Virgie, swallowed a button that
same day – later on – and that *happened*, it seems
like still, but not this. And not a word's been
spoke out loud, for Snowdie's sake, so I trust the
rest of the world will be as careful.   65

You can talk about a baby swallowing a button off a shirt and having to be up-ended and her behind pounded, and it sounds reasonable if you can just see the baby – there she runs – but get to talking about something that's only a kind of *near* thing – and hold your horses.

Well, Hallowe'en, about three o'clock, I was over at Snowdie's helping her cut out patterns – she's kept on sewing for those boys. Me, I have a little girl to sew for – she was right there, asleep on the bed in the next room – and it hurts my conscience being that lucky over Snowdie too. And the twins wouldn't play out in the yard that day but had hold of the scraps and the scissors and the paper of pins and all, and there underfoot they were dressing up and playing ghosts and boogers. Uppermost in their little minds was Hallowe'en.

They had on their masks, of course, tied on over their Buster Brown bobs and pressing a rim around the back. I was used to how they looked by then – but I don't like masks. They both come from Spight's store and cost a nickel. One was the Chinese kind, all yellow and mean with slant eyes and a dreadful thin mustache of black horsy hair.

The other one was a lady, with an almost scary-sweet smile on her lips. I never did take to that smile, with all day for it. Eugene Hudson wanted to be the Chinaman and so Lucius Randall had to be the lady.

So they were making tails and do-lollies and all kinds of foolishness, and sticking them on to their little middles and behinds, snatching every scrap from the shirts and flannels me and Snowdie was cutting out on the dining room table. Sometimes we could grab a little boy and baste something up on him whether or no, but we didn't really pay them much mind, we was talking about the prices of things for winter, and the funeral of an old maid.

So we never heard the step creak or the porch give, at all. That was a blessing. And if it wasn't for something that come from outside us all to tell about it, I wouldn't have the faith I have that it came about.

But happening along our road – like he does every day – was a real trustworthy nigger. He's one of Mrs Stark's mother's niggers, Old Plez Morgan everybody calls him. Lives down beyond me. The real old kind, that knows everybody since time was. He knows more folks than I do, who they are, and all the *fine* people. If you wanted anybody in Morgana that wouldn't be likely to make a mistake in who a person is, you would ask for Old Plez.

So he was making his way down the road, by stages. He still has to do a few people's yards won't let him go, like Mrs Stark, because he don't pull up things. He's no telling how old and starts early and takes his time coming home in the evening – always stopping to speak to people to ask after their health and tell them good evening all the way. Only that day, he said he didn't see a soul *else* – besides you'll hear who in a minute – on the way, not on porches or in the yards. I can't tell you why, unless it was those little gusts of north wind that had started blowing. Nobody likes that.

But yonder ahead of him was walking a man. Plez said it was a white man's walk and a walk he knew – but it struck him it was from away in another year, another time. It wasn't just the walk of anybody supposed to be going along the road to MacLain right at that *time* – and yet it was too – and if it was, he still couldn't think what business that somebody would be up to. That was the careful way Plez was putting it to his mind.

If you saw Plez, you'd know it was him. He had some roses stuck in his hat that day, I saw him right after it happened. Some of Miss Lizzie's fall roses, big as a man's fist and red as blood – they were nodding side-to-side out of the band of his old black hat, and some other little scraps out of the garden laid around the brim, throwed away by Mrs Stark; he'd been cleaning out her beds that day, it was fixing to rain.

He said later he wasn't in any great hurry, or he would have maybe caught up and passed the man. Up yonder ahead he went, going the same way Plez was going, and not much more interested in a race. And a real familiar stranger.

So Plez says presently the familiar stranger paused. It was in front of the MacLains' – and sunk his weight on one leg and just stood there, posey as statues, hand on his hip. Ha! Old Plez says, according, he just leaned himself against the Presbyterian Church gate and waited a while.

Next thing, the stranger – oh, it was King! By then Plez was calling him Mr King to himself – went up through the yard and then didn't go right in like anybody else. First he looked around. He took in the yard and summerhouse and skimmed from cedar to cedar along the edge of where he lived, and under the fig tree at the back and under the wash (if he'd counted it!) and come close to the front again, sniffy like, and Plez said though he couldn't swear to seeing from the Presbyterian Church exactly what Mr King was doing, he knows as good as seeing it that he looked through the blinds. He would have looked in the dining room – have mercy. We shut the West out of Snowdie's eyes of course.

At last he come full front again, around the flowers under the front bedroom. Then he settled himself nice and started up the front steps.

The middle step sings when it's stepped on, but we didn't hear it. Plez said, well, he had on fine tennis shoes. So he got across the front porch and what do you think he's fixing to do but knock on that door? Why wasn't he satisfied with outdoors?

On his own front door. He makes a little shadow knock, like trying to see how it would look, and then puts his present behind his coat. Of course he had something there in a box for her. You know he constitutionally brought home the kind of presents that break your heart. He stands there with one leg out pretty, to surprise them. And I bet a nice smile on his face. Oh, don't ask me to go on!

Suppose Snowdie'd took a notion to glance down the hall – the dining room's at the end of it, and the folding-doors pushed back – and seen him, all 'Come-kiss-me' like that. I don't know if she could have seen that good – but *I* could. I was a fool and didn't look.

It was the twins seen him. Through those little bitty mask holes, those eagle eyes! There ain't going to be no stopping those twins. And he didn't get to knock on the door, but he had his hand raised the second time and his knuckles sticking up, and out come the children on him, hollering 'Boo!' and waving their arms up and down the way it would scare you to death, or it ought to, if you wasn't ready for them.

We heard them charge out, but we thought it was just a nigger that was going by for them to scare, if we thought anything.

Plez says – allowing for all human mistakes – he seen on one side of King come rolling out

Lucius Randall all dressed up, and on the other side, Eugene Hudson all dressed up. Could I have forgotten to speak of their being on skates? Oh, that was all afternoon. They're real good skaters, the little fellows, not to have a sidewalk. They sailed out the door and circled around their father, flying their arms and making their fingers go scary, and those little Buster Brown bobs going in a circle.

Lucius Randall, Plez said, had on something pink, and he did, the basted flannelette teddy-bears we had tried on on top of his clothes and he got away. And said Eugene was a Chinaman, and that was what he was. It would be hard to tell which would come at you the more outrageous of the two, but to me it would be Lucius Randall with the girl's face and the big white cotton gloves falling off his fingers, and oh! he had on *my hat*. This one I milk in.

And they made a tremendous uproar with their skates, Plez said, and that was no mistake, because I remember what a hard time Snowdie and me had hearing what each other had to say all afternoon.

Plez said King stood it a minute – he got to

turning around too. They were skating around him and saying in high birdie voices, 'How do you do, Mister Booger?' You know if children *can* be monkeys, they're going to be them. (Without the masks, though, those two children would have been more polite about it – there's enough Hudson in them.) Skating around and around their papa, and just as ignorant! Poor little fellows. After all, they'd had nobody to scare all day for Hallowe'en, except one or two niggers that went by, and the Y. & M. V. train whistling through at two-fifteen, they scared that.

But monkeys –! Skating around their papa. Plez said if those children had been black, he wouldn't hesitate to say they would remind a soul of little nigger cannibals in the jungle. When they got their papa in their ring-around-a-rosy and he couldn't get out, Plez said it was enough to make an onlooker a little uneasy, and he called once or twice on the Lord. And after they went around high, they crouched down and went around low, about his knees.

The minute come, when King just couldn't get out quick enough. Only he had a hard time, and took him more than one try. He gathered himself together and King is a man of six foot height and weighs like a horse, but he was confused, I take it. But he got aloose and up and out like the Devil was after him – or in him – finally. Right up over the bannister and the ferns, and down the yard and over the ditch and gone. He plowed into the rough toward the Big Black, and the willows waved behind him, and where he run then, Plez don't know and I don't and don't nobody.

Plez said King passed right by him, that time, but didn't seem to know him, and the opportunity had gone by then to speak. And where he run then, nobody knows.

He should have wrote another note, instead of coming.

Well then, the children, I reckon, just held openmouth behind him, and then something got to mounting up after it was all over, and scared them. They come back in the dining room. There were innocent ladies visiting with each other. The little boys had to scowl and frown and drag their skates over the carpet and follow us around the table where we was cutting out Eugene Hudson's underbody, and pull on our skirts till we saw.

74   'Well, speak,' said their mother, and they told

her a booger had come up on the front porch and when they went out to see him he said, 'I'm going. You stay,' so they chased him down the steps and run him off. 'But he looked back like this!' Lucius Randall said, lifting off his mask and showing us on his little naked face with the round blue eyes. And Eugene Hudson said the booger took a handful of pecans before he got through the gate.

And Snowdie dropped her scissors on the mahogany, and her hand just stayed in the air as still, and she looked at me, a look a minute long. At first she caught her apron to her and then started shedding it in the hall while she run to the door — so as not to be caught in it, I suppose, if anybody was still there. She run and the little glass prisms shook in the parlor – I don't remember another time, from *her*. She didn't stop at the door but run on through it and out on the porch, and she looked both ways and was running down the steps. And she run out in the yard and stood there holding to the tree, looking towards the country, but I could tell by the way her head held there wasn't nobody.

When I got to the steps – I didn't like to follow

right away – there was nobody at all but old Plez, who was coming by raising his hat.

'Plez, did you see a gentleman come up on my porch just now?' I heard Snowdie call, and there was Plez, just ambling by with his hat raised, like he was just that minute passing, like we thought. And Plez, of course, he said, 'No'm, Mistis, I don't recollect one soul pass me, whole way from town.'

The little fellows held on to me, I could feel them tugging. And my little girl slept through it all, inside, and then woke up to swallow that button.

Outdoors the leaves were rustling, different from when I'd went in. It was coming on a rain. The day had a two-way look, like a day will at change of the year – clouds dark and the gold air still in the road, and the trees lighter than the sky was. And the oak leaves scuttling and scattering, blowing against Old Plez and brushing on him, the old man.

'You're real positive, I guess, Plez?' asks Snowdie, and he answers comforting-like to her, '*You* wasn't looking for nobody to come today, was

you?'

It was later on that Mrs Stark got hold of Plez and got the truth out of him, and I heard it after a while, through her church. But of course he wasn't going to let Miss Snowdie MacLain get hurt now, after we'd all watched her so long. So he fabricated.

After he'd gone by, Snowdie just stood there in the cool without a coat, with her face turned towards the country and her fingers pulling at little threads on her skirt and turning them loose in the wind, making little kind deeds of it, till I went and got her. She didn't cry.

'Course, could have been a ghost,' Plez told Mrs Stark, 'but a ghost – I believe – if he had come to see the lady of the house, would have waited to have a word with her.'

And he said he had nary doubt in his mind, that it was Mr King MacLain, starting home once more and thinking better of it. Miss Lizzie said to the church ladies, 'I, for one, trust the Negro. I trust him the way you trust me, old Plez's mind has remained clear as a bell. I trust his story implicitly,' she says, 'because that's just what I *know* King MacLain'd do – run.' And that's one time I feel in agreement about something with Miss Lizzie Stark, though she don't know about it, I guess.

And I live and hope *he* hit a stone and fell down running, before he got far off from here, and took the skin off his handsome nose, the devil.

And so that's why Snowdie comes to get her butter now, and won't let me bring it to her any longer. I think she kind of holds it against me, because I was there that day when he come; and she don't like my baby any more.

And you know, Fate says maybe King did know it was Hallowe'en. Do you think he'd go that far for a prank? And his own come back to him? Fate's usually more down to earth than that.

With men like King, your thoughts are bottomless. He was going like the wind, Plez swore to Miss Lizzie Stark; though he couldn't swear to the direction – so he changed and said.

But I bet my little Jersey calf King tarried long enough to get him a child somewhere.

What makes me say a thing like that? I wouldn't say it to my husband, you mind you forget it.

Where is the Voice Coming From?

1963

I says to my wife, 'You can reach and turn it off. You don't have to set and look at a black nigger face no longer than you want to, or listen to what you don't want to hear. It's still a free country.'

I reckon that's how I give myself the idea.

I says, I could find right exactly where in Thermopylae that nigger's living that's asking for equal time. And without a bit of trouble to me.

And I ain't saying it might not be because that's pretty close to where *I* live. The other hand, there could be reasons you might have yourself for knowing how to get there in the dark. It's where you all go for the thing you want when you want it the most. Ain't that right?

The Branch Bank sign tells you in lights, all night long even, what time it is and how hot. When it was quarter to four, and 92, that was me going by in my brother-in-law's truck. He don't deliver nothing at that hour of the morning.

So you leave Four Corners and head west on 79

Nathan B. Forrest Road, past the Surplus & Salvage, not much beyond the Kum Back Drive-In and Trailer Camp, not as far as where the signs starts saying 'Live Bait', 'Used Parts', 'Fireworks', 'Peaches', and 'Sister Peebles Reader and Adviser'. Turn before you hit the city limits and duck back towards the IC tracks. And his street's been paved.

And there was his light on, waiting for me. In his garage, if you please. His car's gone. He's out planning still some other ways to do what we tell 'em they can't. I *thought* I'd beat him home. All I had to do was pick my tree and walk in close behind it.

I didn't come expecting not to wait. But it was so hot, all I did was hope and pray one or the other of us wouldn't melt before it was over.

Now, it wasn't no bargain I'd struck.

I've heard what you've heard about Goat Dykeman, in Mississippi. Sure, everybody knows about Goat Dykeman. Goat he got word to the Governor's Mansion he'd go up yonder and shoot that nigger Meredith clean out of school, if he's let out of the pen to do it. Old Ross turned *that* over in his mind before saying him nay, it stands to reason.

I ain't no Goat Dykeman, I ain't in no pen, and

I ain't ask no Governor Barnett to give me one thing. Unless he wants to give me a pat on the back for the trouble I took this morning. But he don't have to if he don't want to. I done what I done for my own pure-D satisfaction.

As soon as I heard wheels, I knowed who was coming. That was him and bound to be him. It was the right nigger heading in a new white car up his driveway towards his garage with the light shining, but stopping before he got there, may be not to wake 'em. That was him. I knowed it when he cut off the car lights and put his foot out and I knowed him standing dark against the light. I knowed him then like I know me now. I knowed him even by his still, listening back.

Never seen him before, never seen him since, never seen anything of his black face but his picture, never seen his face alive, any time at all, or anywheres, and didn't want to, need to, never hope to see that face and never will. As long as there was no question in my mind.

He had to be the one. He stood right still and waited against the light, his back was fixed, fixed on me like a preacher's eyeballs when he's yelling 'Are you saved?' He's the one.

I'd already brought up my rifle, I'd already taken my sights. And I'd already got him, because it was too late then for him or me to turn by one hair.

Something darker than him, like the wings of a bird, spread on his back and pulled him down. He climbed up once, like a man under bad claws, and like just blood could weigh a ton he walked with it on his back to better light. Didn't get no further than his door. And fell to stay.

He was down. He was down, and a ton load of bricks on his back wouldn't have laid any heavier. There on his paved driveway, yes sir.

And it wasn't till the minute before, that the mockingbird had quit singing. He'd been singing up my sassafras tree. Either he was up early, or he hadn't never gone to bed, he was like me. And the mocker he'd stayed right with me, filling the air till come the crack, till I turned loose of my load. I was like him. I was on top of the world myself. For once.

I stepped to the edge of his light there, where he's laying flat. I says, 'Roland? There was one way left, for me to be ahead of you and stay ahead of you, by Dad, and I just taken it. Now I'm alive and you ain't. We ain't never now, never going to be equals and you know why? One of us is dead. What about that, Roland?' I said. 'Well, you seen to it, didn't you?'

I stood a minute – just to see would somebody inside come out long enough to pick him up. And there she comes, the woman. I doubt she'd been to sleep. Because it seemed to me she'd been in there keeping awake all along.

It was mighty green where I skint over the yard getting back. That nigger wife of his, she wanted nice grass! I bet my wife would hate to pay her water bill. And for burning her electricity. And there's my brother-in-law's truck, still waiting with the door open. 'No Riders' – that didn't mean me.

There wasn't a thing I been able to think of since would have made it to go any nicer. Except a chair to my back while I was putting in my waiting. But going home, I seen what little time it takes after all to get a thing done like you really want it. It was 4.34, and while I was looking it moved to 35. And the temperature stuck where it was. All that night I guarantee you it had stood without dropping, a good 92. 83

My wife says, 'What? Didn't the skeeters bite you?' She said, 'Well, they been asking that – why somebody didn't trouble to load a rifle and get some of these agitators out of Thermopylae. Didn't the fella keep drumming it in, what a good idea? The one that writes a column ever' day?'

I says to my wife, 'Find *some* way I don't get the credit.'

'He says do it for Thermopylae,' she says. 'Don't you ever skim the paper?'

I says, 'Thermopylae never done nothing for me. And I don't owe nothing to Thermopylae. Didn't do it for you. Hell, any more'n I'd do something or other for them Kennedys! I done it for my own pure-D satisfaction.'

'It's going to get him right back on TV,' says my wife. 'You watch for the funeral.'

I says, 'You didn't even leave a light burning when you went to bed. So how was I supposed to even get me home or pull Buddy's truck up safe in our front yard?'

'Well, hear another good joke on you,' my wife says next. 'Didn't you hear the news? The N double ACP is fixing to send somebody to Thermopylae. Why couldn't you waited? You might could have got you somebody better. Listen and hear 'em say so.'

I ain't but one. I reckon you have to tell *somebody*.

'Where's the gun, then?' my wife says. 'What did you do with our protection?'

I says, 'It was scorching! It was scorching!' I told her, 'It's laying out on the ground in rank weeds, trying to cool off, that's what it's doing now.'

'You dropped it,' she says. 'Back there.'

And I told her, 'Because I'm so tired of ever'thing in the world being just that hot to the touch! The keys to the truck, the doorknob, the bed-sheet, ever'thing, it's all like a stove lid. There just ain't much going that's worth holding on to it no more,' I says, 'when it's a hundred and two in the shade by day and by night not too much difference. I wish *you*'d laid *your* finger to that gun.'

'Trust you to come off and leave it,' my wife says.

'Is that how no-'count I am?' she makes me ask. '*You* want to go back and get it?'

'You're the one they'll catch. I say it's so hot

that even if you get to sleep you wake up feeling like you cried all night!' says my wife. 'Cheer up, here's one more joke before time to get up. Heard what *Caroline* said? Caroline said, "Daddy, I just can't wait to grow up big, so I can marry *James Meredith*." I heard that where I work. One rich-bitch to another one, to make her cackle.'

'At least I kept some dern teen-ager from North Thermopylae getting there and doing it first,' I says. 'Driving his own car.'

On TV and in the paper, they don't know but half of it. They know who Roland Summers was without knowing who I am. His face was in front of the public before I got rid of him, and after I got rid of him there it is again – the same picture. And none of me. I ain't ever had one made. Not ever! The best that newspaper could do for me was offer a five-hundred-dollar reward for finding out who I am. For as long as they don't know who that is, whoever shot Roland is worth a good deal more right now than Roland is.

But by the time I was moving around uptown, it was hotter still. That pavement in the middle of
Main Street was so hot to my feet I might've been

walking the barrel of my gun. If the whole world could've just felt Main Street this morning through the soles of my shoes, maybe it would've helped some.

Then the first thing I heard 'em say was the N double ACP done it themselves, killed Roland Summers, and proved it by saying the shooting was done by a expert (I hope to tell you it was!) and at just the right hour and minute to get the whites in trouble.

You can't win.

'They'll never find him,' the old man trying to sell roasted peanuts tells me to my face.

And it's so hot.

It looks like the town's on fire already, which-ever ways you turn, ever' street you strike, because there's those trees hanging them pones of bloom like split watermelon. And a thousand cops crowding ever'where you go, half of 'em too young to start shaving, but all streaming sweat alike. I'm getting tired of 'em.

I was already tired of seeing a hundred cops getting us white people nowheres. Back at the beginning, I stood on the corner and I watched them new babyface cops loading nothing but nigger children into the paddy wagon and they come marching out of a little parade and into the paddy wagon singing. And they got in and sat down without providing a speck of trouble, and their hands held little new American flags, and all the cops could do was knock them flagsticks a-loose from their hands, and not let 'em pick 'em up, that was all, and give 'em a free ride. And children can just get 'em more flags.

Everybody: It don't get you nowhere to take nothing from nobody unless you make sure it's for keeps, for good and all, for ever and amen.

I won't be sorry to see them brickbats hail down on us for a change. Pop bottles too, they can come flying whenever they want to. Hundreds, all to smash, like Birmingham. I'm waiting on 'em to bring out them switchblade knives, like Harlem and Chicago. Watch TV long enough and you'll see it all to happen on Deacon Street in Thermopylae. What's holding it back, that's all? – Because it's *in* 'em.

I'm ready myself for that funeral.

Oh, they may find me. May catch me one day in spite of 'emselves. (But I grew up in the country.) May try to railroad me into the electric chair, and what that amounts to is something hotter than yesterday and today put together.

But I advise 'em to go careful. Ain't it about time us taxpayers starts to calling the moves? Starts to tell the teachers *and* the preachers *and* the judges of our so-called courts how far they can go?

Even the President so far, he can't walk in my house without being invited, like he's my daddy, just to say whoa. Not yet!

Once, I run away from my home. And there was a ad for me, come to be printed in our county weekly. My mother paid for it. It was from her. It says: 'SON: You are not being hunted for anything but to find you.' That time, I come on back home.

But people are dead now.

And it's so hot. Without it even being August yet.

Anyways, I seen him fall. I was evermore the one.

So I reach me down my old guitar off the nail in the wall. 'Cause I've got my guitar, what I've held on to from way back when, and I never dropped that, never lost or forgot it, never hocked it but to get it again, never give it away, and I set in my chair, with nobody home but me, and I start to play, and sing a-down. And sing a-down, down, down, down. Sing a-down, down, down, down. Down.

READ MORE IN PENGUIN

For complete information about books available from Penguin and how to order them, please write to us at the appropriate address below. Please note that for copyright reasons the selection of books varies from country to country.

IN THE UNITED KINGDOM: Please write to *Dept. JC, Penguin Books Ltd, FREEPOST, West Drayton, Middlesex UB7 0BR.*

If you have any difficulty in obtaining a title, please send your order with the correct money, plus ten per cent for postage and packaging, to *PO Box No. 11, West Drayton, Middlesex UB7 0BR.*

IN THE UNITED STATES: Please write to *Consumer Sales, Penguin USA, P.O. Box 999, Dept. 17109, Bergenfield, New Jersey 07621-0120.* VISA and MasterCard holders call 1-800-253-6476 to order all Penguin titles.

IN CANADA: Please write to *Penguin Books Canada Ltd, 10 Alcorn Avenue, Suite 300, Toronto, Ontario M4V 3B2.*

IN AUSTRALIA: Please write to *Penguin Books Australia Ltd, P.O. Box 257, Ringwood, Victoria 3134.*

IN NEW ZEALAND: Please write to *Penguin Books (NZ) Ltd, Private Bag 102902, North Shore Mail Centre, Auckland 10.*

IN INDIA: Please write to *Penguin Books India Pvt Ltd, 706 Eros Apartments, 56 Nehru Place, New Delhi 110 019.*

IN THE NETHERLANDS: Please write to *Penguin Books Netherlands bv, Postbus 3507, NL-1001 AH Amsterdam.*

IN GERMANY: Please write to *Penguin Books Deutschland GmbH, Metzlerstrasse 26, 60594 Frankfurt am Main.*

IN SPAIN: Please write to *Penguin Books S. A., Bravo Murillo 19, 1o B, 28015 Madrid.*

IN ITALY: Please write to *Penguin Italia s.r.l., Via Felice Casati 20, I-20124 Milano.*

IN FRANCE: Please write to *Penguin France S. A., 17 rue Lejeune, F-31000 Toulouse.*

IN JAPAN: Please write to *Penguin Books Japan, Ishikiribashi Building, 2-5-4, Suido, Bunkyo-ku, Tokyo 112.*

IN GREECE: Please write to *Penguin Hellas Ltd, Dimocritou 3, GR-106 71 Athens.*

IN SOUTH AFRICA: Please write to *Longman Penguin Southern Africa (Pty) Ltd, Private Bag X08, Bertsham 2013.*